Peas for Princes
by Lucina M. Huff

Copyright 2021 Lucina M. Huff

ISBN: 9798733734477
Imprint: Independently published

Cover design by RK Creative Studio

Other Titles by Lucina M. Huff:
The Book of Memories

For Maggie

Peas for Princes

Once upon a time, there lived a strong and intelligent princess named Myra Wellington. For many years, she searched for a prince because she wanted one. Not because the law forced her to marry, nor because she was too weak to rule on her own. Not to save herself or her loved ones from a curse or other danger. And not because her parents were forcing her to form an advantageous political alliance, either. She wanted to marry because she knew that finding a life partner would give her a different kind of strength, for she had seen the beauty of true partnership from her parents. However, Myra knew he had to be a true prince.

But what made a real prince? Certainly not his title. She'd met many "princes" in her search. They all ended up being false. Not his outward beauty, either. Looks would change or decline with age. Though, she would readily admit that personal attraction was necessary. No, a true prince had something else. Something indefinable and elusive. In all the would-be princes she'd met, something always seemed not quite right. In the end, she decided it must be her that wasn't quite right and gave up.

Until the year of her twenty-third birthday, when her parents started acting suspicious.

After trying to catch her parents for months during the summit preparations, Myra finally cornered her mother early in the morning of arrival day.

"What are you and Father up to? You usually include me in all the planning. Why did you leave me out of this?" Angry tears threatened to spill down her cheeks. "And why did you choose a date so near my birthday?"

Her mother set a large, bow-wrapped dress box down on Myra's dressing table. She took ahold of her daughter's hands and gave them a gentle pat.

"Don't worry, darling. You'll find out soon enough. In the meantime, here's an early birthday gift. Be sure to hurry to the receiving room." The queen kissed her daughter's cheek and left.

Myra sat at her dressing table with a huff. She glared at the dress box and tugged on the bow. After a moment, she removed the lid and pulled the dress out, holding it up. She smiled at the floral pattern, the short sleeves, and the mid-calf length. It was unusual and unrestrictive. Her mother knew her well. Her eye caught on something remaining in the box. She took that out, too and laughed at the matching shorts. It's not that she hated dresses, but everyone in the castle knew how much she preferred the movement of trousers and split skirts.

A knock on her door brought a light breakfast and a string of ladies' maids to dress and prepare her for the long day ahead.

*****

Myra stepped through the doorway into the near-empty receiving room. A chamberlain on the inside cleared his throat.

"Presenting Her Highness, Myra Astrid Wellington, Crown Princess of Wellington," he boomed.

Noting his partner stationed at the doorway across the room, she stepped close to him and whispered, "Please tell me that's not going to happen *every* time I re-enter the room today?"

"Yes, milady."

She clenched and unclenched her fists. "Isn't that a bit extreme?"

He ducked his head and mumbled, "I'm sorry, milady. It's our duty."

"For everyone?"

"Yes, milady."

"I see." She nodded. Sighed. "Carry on."

She joined her parents at the row of picture windows, linking arms with her mother. The windows supplied a view of the front approach to the castle, making it an excellent place to watch for arriving guests. They didn't have to wait long for the first, and as they were greeting one another, the next guest arrived and so on, until there was a small gathering mingling happily throughout the receiving room.

2

At a lull in the arrivals, Myra slipped back over to the windows. She wanted to look at the larger picture to see if she was imagining the trend in the composition of the attendees. It was still early, but she may have figured out why her parents had been acting like giddy schoolchildren during the summit preparations. Most, if not all, of the rulers that would usually attend a summit personally had sent a representative instead —a young male representative, to be precise. She sighed, massaging her forehead, and turned to stare out the window.

Another young man arrived, riding a large brown pony, the first to travel without an entourage. Myra smirked. He sprang off his pony, laughing as he handed the reins to the waiting footman. He removed a bandolier of throwing knives and passed them to the footman as well, talking and laughing all the while. A bundle of dark grey clouds emerged overhead, blocking the sun. The young man grabbed an umbrella from behind his saddle, opened it, and gave it to the footman. He then skipped up the stairs. A sound of amusement escaped her lips. She whipped around, checking if anyone caught her. Safely alone —and seeing her parents occupied with other guests— she moved to the entrance.

The newest arrival stopped to confer with the entrance chamberlain, giving Myra the chance for a closer look. His long hair —captured at the nape of his neck— was the same color as his pony. Surprisingly, the newcomer was of a height with her and slim in a way that suggested he was built for speed. She was dying to know if he really knew how to use those knives, or if they were only for show.

The chamberlain cleared his throat. "Presenting my Lord, Noah Fawx, Cousin of Her Excellency, the Empress of Wriddannia."

Myra stepped up, extending her hand in greeting. He took her hand and bowed over it.

"I'm Myra Wellington. Welcome to the summit."

As he straightened, he kissed her hand and winked. "It's my pleasure to attend." He winked again. "Everyone calls me Fawx."

She felt the callouses on the hand he still held and stared into his laughing golden brown eyes. She quirked an eyebrow. "I'm sure they do." She glanced towards their still-clasped hands. "Are you going to hold that all day?"

He grinned, highlighting his freckles, and turned his hand, holding hers tighter. He gave a gentle tug and pulled her towards the buffet tables, laughing —and talking— the entire way.

"When was the last time you ate, Myra? My cousin woke me before dawn, then shoved me out the door before I had the chance to even smell breakfast. She was so sure I would be late, but look," he gestured at the windows, "it's not even midday!"

Myra laughed as she let herself be pulled along. "Wait. Did you say you left this morning?"

He nodded, mouth full.

"How in the world did you arrive so quickly?"

Fawx chuckled and winked. "I took the shortest, most direct route. Naturally."

Myra's face scrunched as she thought over all the maps. "I give up. Which route is that?"

He sipped his chilled cider and answered with a sly grin. "Across the river and through the forest."

She gasped. "Isn't the forest deadly?"

In two blinks of an eye, he slipped a hidden knife out, twirled it, and returned it. "Only for the unprepared."

He returned his attention to the food and she mumbled, "Guess that solves that question."

Fawx tilted his head back towards her, one corner of his mouth lifted, eyes sparkling. "What was that, Myyy-RA?"

One hand covered her mouth as she giggled. "You really are a fox, aren't you?"

He grinned and bowed. "At your service."

The entrance chamberlain again cleared his throat. "Presenting my Lord, Soren Andersen, Nephew of Grand Archon Marius."

4

Myra's gaze drifted toward the door, inspecting the latest arrival. Her eyes locked with his and her body froze. Her heart thudded in her chest. Detached, she catalogued him from head to toe. *Tall and thin. Dark hair, dark eyes, dark clothes. Devilishly handsome.* He blinked, Fawx nudged her shoulder, and the spell was —gratefully— broken. No one approached him. With one long blink, she shook herself and rallied.

Within two steps, Fawx caught up to her. "Going to greet the magician's nephew?"

She merely nodded.

"Beware the Fruitless Frost," he whispered in her ear. He kissed her cheek, winked, and dashed off.

Stunned, she watched Fawx for a moment, bounding and twisting, laughing and talking through the crowd. She huffed through her nose. She'd have to keep an eye on that one.

The princess smiled at Soren Andersen and held out her hand. "Hello. I'm Myra Wellington. Welcome to the summit."

He shook her hand. "Soren. Pleased to make your acquaintance, Your Highness."

The velvety softness of his voice nearly caused her to miss the catlike qualities in his smile. Her heart thumped on alert.

"Call me Myra."

She motioned for him to join her in the room. He bowed his head in acceptance.

"As you wish, my lady."

She arched an eyebrow.

". . . Myra."

Fawx darted across her line of sight and a surge of curiosity washed over her. "Soren, do you know why the Grand Archon wasn't able to attend?"

He grinned his cat-smile. "Apologies, my. . . Myra. As to matters pertaining to my uncle, I don't question. I humbly obey." A muscle in his jaw twitched.

Her stomach quivered and the hair on the back of her neck stood on end.

"Presenting," —the chamberlain's loud voice startled her— "His Highness, Owain Price, Prince of Glasmor."

Once again, Myra was captivated, although for an entirely different reason. Whereas Soren's dark beauty whispered of possible danger, this prince shone with the light of an angel. The door behind him shut, cutting off the midday sun, and he returned to the realm of mortals. She laughed at herself. His "halo" had been a trick of the light shining through his blonde hair.

Fawx dashed up, grabbing and tugging her hand. "Oh, goody, goody. His Gracelessness has arrived. Let's go greet him." He pulled her away from Soren, and muttered to himself, "I want to know if he's still cursed."

She glanced back towards Soren with an apologetic shrug, then turned to Fawx. "Do you know everybody?"

"Of course, Myra." The way he lilted her name, accenting the last syllable while drawing out the first, was a bit endearing. "My cousin's the Empress. It's my job to know everyone." He winked.

Myra chuckled and slipped her hand out of his grip. When he flashed her a pout, she threw him a wink of her own.

She stepped up beside her father, who was greeting Prince Owain. Her father made the proper introductions and she curtsied.

"When my brother informed me that he would be sending me here, I did not expect to meet such a lovely young lady as yourself, Your Highness," Owain said.

"Nor did I expect to be surrounded by so many handsome young gentlemen." The princess smiled. "And please, call me Myra."

With raised eyebrows, Owain's blue eyes cut to her father and back. "Oh, then were you not aware of the plan?"

She scowled. "What plan?"

Her father hemmed and hawed. He put his arm around her shoulder, pulling her off to one side. "Now, Myra, your mother and I . . ."

Fawx skipped up and bowed to the King. "Your Majesty, if I may. Fawx, at your service. May we borrow Myra to settle a dispute we're having?"

6

As Fawx motioned between himself and another, Myra glanced behind her to find Soren, of all people. As curious as she was to find out what those two could be arguing about, she was infinitely more eager to learn her parents' plans.

The corners of her father's eyes crinkled with his smile and he patted her shoulder. "Go on then, dear. These lads need your company more than I do."

"But Father, you were in the middle of explaining—"

"There will be plenty of time for explanations later," he cut her off. Nodding behind her, he said, "Our guests are waiting for you."

Then her father turned her around by the shoulders and gave her a little shove —straight into the trio of young men. Off-balance, she bumped into Owain, knocking him backwards. He backstepped, tripping on the edge of a rug. Pinwheeling his arms in a futile attempt to arrest his fall, his rump hit the ground with a soft thud. Above him, Myra looked on in dismay, saved from a similar fate by Fawx and Soren who had each grabbed one of her arms.

Fawx grinned at the fallen prince. "I'd say that's a yes."

Sufficiently steady, Myra shrugged out of Fawx and Soren's hold. She bent down to check on Owain.

"I'm so sorry, Your Highness. Are you all right?" She reached toward him.

He scuttled away from her and into a pedestal holding a flower arrangement. The vase wobbled and toppled, spilling flowers and water on his head. She moved towards him again.

"Stop! Don't come any closer, please." His lips smiled, but his eyes begged, and his chest heaved. "There is no need to apologize. It happens all the time." He finally regained his feet and placed the empty vase upright on the pedestal. "Also, if I am going to address you informally, you should do the same with me."

He ran a hand back through his wet hair, giving her a smoldering look. Behind her, Fawx snickered. Myra held in her own snicker and waved over a couple servants: one to clean the mess, the other to take Owain to his room.

When Owain was out of earshot, Fawx rubbed his hands together. "Well, that was exciting. Don't you think so, Myra?"

"I wouldn't say that 'exciting' was the correct word," Soren said.

Fawx huffed, fists on hips. "Well then, what word would *you* use, oh Great Frosty One?"

Soren's jaw clenched so tight, Myra could hear his teeth grinding together. His tone remained as light and velvety as ever, though. "Amusing, diverting, or delightful, perhaps."

Instead of admitting that he agreed with Soren, Fawx sneered and jerked his head away, pouting at the ground. Looking back and forth between the two of them, Myra laughed. She took ahold of each of them by an arm and started mingling with the other guests. She'd decided it was best not to leave the two of them alone with each other, but she didn't want to play favorites, either. It didn't take long for Owain to rejoin them, maintaining a noticeable distance from her. Every so often, she shot him a questioning glance, to which his only response was a shrug and a smile.

After a couple hours with her charming trio, Myra excused herself to the wash facilities. She stopped in the doorway on her return, silencing the chamberlain there for the moment. She looked over the room, trying to find her parents. It was way beyond time for them to explain themselves. She spotted her mother and inched forward. Two things happened simultaneously: the chamberlain announced her once again, and Fawx bounded up to collect her, the other two trailing close behind.

She eyed her mother in the distance and sighed internally. Outwardly, she smiled at her self-appointed trio of escorts. They were amusing enough company for the afternoon. Soren and Fawx argued over a thousand trivial nothings, while Owain constantly switched sides in a manner that only made sense to him. She stayed out of it as best she could.

Later at the buffet tables, Myra reached for a glass of chilled cider. However, it happened to be the same glass that Owain reached for. He recoiled, knocking the glass from her hand, toward her face. Soren's quick reflexes saved her from a face full of cider as he pivoted between her and the splashing drink, shielding her with his body. The cider cup shattered as it hit his back, sparkling glass and amber fluid raining to the floor.

Owain winced and backed away several steps. Bowing low, he said, "My humblest apologies to you both." His sky-blue eyes were clouded as he straightened back up. With a sigh, he muttered, "I warned my brother this would happen."

She side-eyed Owain as she stepped around Soren, hands fluttering over his back.

"How do you feel? Are you hurt?"

He pulled her back in front of him, stilling her hands. "I'm not injured, Myra. You have no need to worry over me."

As he stood holding her hands, his velvet voice reassuring her, for the first time in a long time, Myra wanted to find her lifelong prince. Could he be the one? The true prince she'd searched for? How would she know?

A clap of thunder resounded, rattling the windows. She jumped, thoughts interrupted.

"Are you afraid of thunderstorms, Myra?" Soren asked, in his velvet-soft voice.

She shook her head. "No. Just startled." She flashed him and the other two a winning smile. "I haven't been paying any attention to the weather today."

Fawx winked. "That's quite understandable."

She giggled and Soren scoffed. Someone had called a servant over to clean up the cider mess. Looking around the room, she realized most of the guests had retired. She glanced out the windows and her eyes widened. Through the torrents of rain streaming down, she saw only darkness.

"Where did the time go?"

From his two-yard distance, Owain replied, "I'm afraid we have monopolized it, Myra. For better or worse."

Everyone laughed. The pattering rain filled the silence that followed.

Myra swung her hands. "Well, I suppose we should all turn in."

The others rushed to agree and fumbled over each other to bid her goodnight. As they neared the hallway, a pounding on the entrance door halted them. She nodded to the weary chamberlain and he swung open the door. Drenched and dripping, a young man stepped inside and sneezed.

Myra rushed over to the sopping gentleman.

"Who are you?"

He wrapped his arms around himself as he shivered. "R-r-r-Ronan W-w-w-w-Weylyn." He forced the answer out through his chattering teeth.

She looked to the chamberlain, who stiffened.

"The Honorable Ronan Weylyn, Taran of Dinas Tov," the chamberlain stated, wide-eyed.

A flock of servants arrived with blankets and warm beverages. She took the stack of blankets and plopped them in Soren's hands, assessing her charming trio. Two were clearly there to help, but Owain was at his usual distance, scuffing his feet along the ground. She dismissed him for the night. She caught Fawx's eye and motioned to the beverage tray. He jumped to prepare the tea.

As she wrapped blankets around the sneezing Taran, she ordered, "Soren, bring a chair, please."

He thumped down the nearest chair —an overstuffed, plush armchair.

With a sneeze, the soaked man protested. "I couldn't possibly sit in such a lovely chair in this state. I'd ruin it."

"Nonsense. How long have you been on your feet in this rain, Your Honor?" Myra stared him down.

"As long as necessary." He stared back, unruffled.

She pushed him into the chair and roughly handed him a cup of tea. "Drink this slowly. When it's gone, the servants will show you to your rooms." She gathered up her followers and shooed them away. "I'm Myra, by the way. Myra Wellington. I'll introduce these fools," she smiled, "to you in the morning."

"Myra," he called to her as she left. "Thank you for your kindness. And please, call me Ronan."

She smiled and nodded.

In the hallway, Fawx caught her by the arm, stopping her for a moment. He whispered, "Don't be too hard on His Gracelessness. He's the one who rallied the servants and suggested we all go help you."

After imparting that bit of intel, he kissed her cheek, winked, and scampered off. Myra stared after him, blinking. What was that little fox up to?

*****

Myra sat by her parents in the dining hall, eating breakfast and watching the room full of men. A couple kept to themselves, but most had formed into lively small groups, probably talking about plans for the summit discussions. Her eyes widened as she caught sight of an oddly familiar grouping. Dark Soren sat calmly smiling beside the shining Owain, while across the table the little Fawx laughed.

Fawx winked when he caught her staring. He tossed an apple and flipped out a knife. Owain's arm snaked across the table and snatched the knife from the air. He stabbed the apple, pulled it off, then slammed the knife down in front of Fawx. She hadn't realized how close they were to her until she heard Owain's scolding words.

"This is not the time for showing off."

"He's correct. There will be plenty of time for that later," Soren added.

"A fair time, when all of us have the chance to flaunt ourselves." Owain grinned and bit into his stolen apple.

Frowning, Myra turned to her parents. But before she could ask them anything, they stood up. She cracked her jaw and breathed out through her nose.

"First off, we'd like to thank you all for joining us in surprising our daughter. As parents, we can't express our gratitude at your indulgence deeply enough," her father began.

Myra's heartbeat quickened. *Surprise?*

Her mother smiled. "We also hope that the next few days will be filled with fun for everyone as we celebrate Myra's birthday together."

Myra's court smile faded as iron claws squeezed her chest. *What the heck is going on?*

Her father continued, "Finish up your breakfasts. Soon we'll begin our activity for the day: your short personal presentations. You'll each have five minutes to show your best selves."

Myra stood, slamming her hands on the table. "What on earth are you talking about? Doesn't the summit start today? Isn't *that* why everyone came?"

Her mother tried to caress her arm, but she flinched away. "No, darling. They came for you. You gave up searching for your perfect prince, so your father and I gathered all these wonderful young gentlemen together for you. If you can't find him here, he probably doesn't exist."

Myra spluttered, pointing in succession. "You . . . they . . . me? Here?"

Her father put his arm around her mother and scratched his graying beard. "Well, my dear, we're not getting any younger, you see. And you had given up. We just wanted to help a little."

"That's right, darling. Now, where's your smile? You may as well enjoy yourself since they're already here."

Fury boiled out in an inarticulate yell. Myra spun around and stormed out. Seething, she headed to the sheep field. She needed the wooly comfort of her outdoor sanctuary. She climbed over the wooden fence, grateful to be wearing her favored trousers. Face buried in the nearest sheep, she scolded Ronan when he approached her.

"Go away! You know you're not supposed to disturb me when I'm here." She'd mistaken him for a shepherd.

"I'm sorry, Myra. I didn't know."

She looked up at her name, cheeks hot. "Oh. It's you."

He nodded and pet the sheep. She sighed loudly several times. He continued patting the sheep. She gritted her teeth

12

and rolled her eyes. The low bleating of the sheep filled the silence.

"Is there something you'd like to say?" Ronan asked.

She sneered. "There are a large number of extremely impolite things I'd love to say, but I suppose the most pressing question I have is: why are you here?"

"In Wellington?"

She snorted and muttered to herself, "No, I know why you're in Wellington. I know why you're *all* in Wellington." She looked up at him and braced herself. "Why are you out here wandering around, instead of preparing for your presentation?"

"I heard the sheep from my bedroom and came out to find them." He sat cross-legged on the grass. "I don't have a presentation to prepare for. I'm on vacation." He stuck his hands behind his head and laid down.

Myra's eye twitched and she massaged her forehead. "Aren't you a part of my parents' scheme like everyone else?"

"I don't believe so."

"But you showed up on the same day."

"I'm terribly sorry about that. It was never my intention to come here." Ronan yawned. "Pardon me. I didn't sleep well last night."

"Oh? Were you still cold from the storm-drenching?"

He shook his head. "The blankets and tea warmed me well."

"Then what was the problem?"

He smiled. It was the first time he'd done so, but she hoped it wouldn't be the last. He'd just revealed a set of hidden dimples.

"It's nothing worth mentioning."

She plopped on the ground beside him. "I'll tell you my troubles, if you tell me yours."

Her efforts were rewarded with laughter.

He rolled onto his side, facing her, head propped on his hand. "I'm really not one to complain of trivial matters, Myra."

13

"Please? I'd love to tackle a solvable problem right now."

He was silent for a moment. "Do you have an *un*solvable one?"

She nodded.

"I don't believe in the unsolvable. Tell me your problem. We'll find a solution together."

She pulled at the grass. "My parents ambushed me this morning in front of everyone. Didn't you see it?"

He shook his head. "When did this happen?"

"At breakfast."

"In the dining hall?" He paused for her confirmation. "I ate in my room and came here when I finished."

She put her chin in her hand and sighed. "I thought we were preparing for a summit, but it turns out that my parents were gathering all the eligible young noblemen to help me find a husband instead."

"Do you not want to find a husband?"

"It's not that, it's. . ." She stood and stalked over to the nearest sheep, fists clenched. "They've turned it into a spectacle. A, a game. And made *me* the center of it." She slumped across the sheep's back. "Besides, how could I possibly find the kind of man I'm looking for in a few days, when I couldn't find him after years of searching?"

"Is that your unsolvable problem?" Ronan asked quietly from his place on the ground.

Myra scratched her head and mumbled, "Maybe. I don't know. I don't see any way to get out of this mess my parents created. Not now that everyone's arrived. I'll be forced to play along." She thumped her head down on the sheep and scratched its neck.

He sat up and tapped his knee. "I can be your inside man, if you'd like. Help you gather information and assess the candidates."

She whipped around. "You'd do that? But, don't you have other plans?"

He shrugged. "A trip to the seaside forced by my advisors." He tipped his head to the side and smiled. "I'd rather stay and help a friend."

She smiled in return. "Wait." Her brows furrowed, thinking over maps. "If you were headed to the seaside, how did you end up here? And on foot?"

The bell tolled and Myra cringed. Her lower lip trembled as she patted the sheep goodbye. Ronan followed her out of the pen, walking with her back inside.

He explained, "Shortly after the storm began, we came across a mother and her four children at the crossroads. I offered them a ride to the nearest town, which happened to be Wellington. After a hot meal, we found that there was only one vacant room. I let them have it. When the innkeeper learned who I was, he sent me here."

"You walked all the way from town in such a storm?"

He looked at her, gaze steady. "My men and the horses were settled for the night."

They walked in silence for a time as Myra contemplated the man beside her. A man who seemed to treat everyone with the same level of care and compassion, be they strangers on the roadside, his own subordinates, or new-met peers. It was a rare find if it turned out to be true.

"Won't your men worry about you?"

He shook his head. "I left word of my whereabouts with the innkeeper. They'll be coming to collect me soon."

"Oh. I thought you had decided to stay." She stared at the gravel walkway.

He stopped. "I'd like to, Myra, but you never accepted my offer of help."

Her eyes lit up as she realized he was returning her power of choice. "Thank you, Ronan. I'd like your help, please, if you don't mind changing your plans."

She smiled. He smiled back, dimples showing, and nodded. They resumed walking.

"Now, then. I believe you had a minor problem last night?" she prodded.

He laughed. "You're not going to let that go, are you?"

"No. You helped me. It's my turn."

He sighed. "It's really nothing. It's just," he looked at her sheepishly, "no matter what I did, I couldn't get comfortable on that bed. It's lumpy and hard." He scratched the side of his nose and finished with a mumble, "It felt like I was sleeping on a bed of rocks."

The princess bit back her laughter. "I'll be sure to pass the word along."

*****

After a mind-numbing day of inane presentations in which grown men strutted around like peacocks, Myra was thrilled for a moment alone with her mother. Until she learned about the hidden test her mother had prepared for the suitors. It took all her self-control not to snap.

Voice toneless, she prodded, "What do you mean you put pea gravel under all the mattresses?"

"It's an old family legend, darling. Tradition that's been passed on for generations. A test for a true prince or princess," the queen answered, all smiles.

Myra ground her jaw. "I don't understand."

Her mother patted her shoulder. "You place a pea under twenty mattresses. Only a true prince or princess can feel it." She grinned. "I substituted with pea gravel and put my own twist on the twenty mattresses. Since we have so many princes to choose from."

Myra spluttered. "You put *rocks* in their beds, and you think they won't be able to tell?"

Her mother nodded vigorously. "Definitely. There were only four who felt them last night, so tonight, I've removed some of the gravel and changed to thicker mattresses. We'll see how the four feel in the morning."

Her mother stared at her, nose crinkled and eyes sparkling. Frustration burning her chest, Myra spun on her heel and left before she would say something hurtful.

*****

Cheerful birdsong woke Myra the following morning. The tweeting birds did not reflect her mood as she dragged herself out of bed, through her dressing room, and into the dining hall for breakfast. Since her parents still refused to share the schedule of events with her, she was left to wonder what new torture they had in store for the day. Thankfully, she had eliminated half of the potential suitors during yesterday's presentations. Although, she saw they were all still hanging around for the show.

Her father stood and cleared his throat. "Today's event is something that we hope everyone will enjoy. It's a team battle simulation we call 'capture the flag'."

She perked up, heart —and mood— lightening.

"There will be five teams of five. The team that has the most flags in their possession at sundown will be the winner." He looked at his daughter. "Myra, will you join the competitors?"

She grinned. "You know I never miss capture the flag."

"Wonderful! The competition area has been prepared and the teams are posted in the hall outside. You have half an hour to gather your gear and meet at the entrance to the back gardens." The king turned to look at the large clock on the wall. When no one moved, he said, "Time starts now. Get going."

Myra scooted her chair away from the table and scampered out to check the list for her teammates. On her team? Ronan, Fawx, Soren, and Owain. She rolled her eyes and bit her cheek to keep from cursing. They must be the four men her mother mentioned last night. The ones who'd felt the rocks in their beds. She knew Ronan had.

The hallway filled with a couple dozen men as the competitors came to check the list. Surrounded, she tried to find a way out while simultaneously searching for any one of her teammates. A newly familiar calloused hand slipped into hers and led her out of the chaos. Fawx winked as he released her hand.

She assessed her team. She knew from the presentations that at least one of them was a highly skilled fighter. The other three had chosen not to showcase any fighting skills.

She took the lead. "Grab your best weapon and a bag, then meet me at the kitchen in ten minutes."

Soren stopped her. "Do we need our armor?"

"No. The battlefield will have a barrier in place."

They scattered. In her room, Myra grabbed her pair of hand scythes, an empty bag, and a coil of rope. She twirled the scythes, loosening her arms and wrists, then kicked a couple imaginary foes to warm-up her legs, too. Satisfied, she dashed to the kitchen, beating everyone except Ronan. She grinned when she saw him holding a rope as well.

"You can never have too much rope," she said, smiling at him.

"I have found that to be false, on more than one occasion," Owain said.

He strode toward them carrying a shining shield, his sword sheathed at his hip. He stopped a good distance from the princess. She still hadn't figured out why he always kept such space between them.

Ronan turned to him. "Why is that?"

Owain answered with a sigh. "It's too easy to become entangled in one's own tool."

Fawx, who had snuck up behind her, chimed in. "His Gracelessness is an expert on getting tangled up in things."

"Owain, pass us your bag and wait here for Soren. When he arrives, you two join us inside the larder." She was done wasting time chatting.

"Have you participated in many simulations, Myra?" Ronan asked.

She grinned and passed hard bread to him and Fawx. "They're one of my favorite pastimes, particularly capture the flag."

"Ah, then we'll have more than just a home terrain advantage." Fawx winked.

18

She nodded and continued handing them travel food items such as cheese and dried meat. She pursed her lips at a box on the top shelf. Ronan reached for it, but Soren stepped inside, blocking him. He handed the box down to Myra with a smile.

"Apologies for my tardiness," he said.

She passed around the dried fruits from the box. "No, I'm sorry for not waiting."

From his place leaning in the doorway, Owain interrupted, "Apologies like that could go on forever."

She tightened her bag and slung it on her back, then rubbed her chin as she looked over her teammates. Fawx, wearing forest green from head to toe, bristled with knives. She checked his shoes and smiled. Soft-soled, as suspected. Soren stood next to him, a towering shadow in all black with a dark, curved sword at his hip. Beside him was Ronan, holding what appeared to be a plain hiking stick. Behind them all, Owain lounged in a sky-blue shirt that matched his eyes holding his shining shield.

Myra scowled and headed out to the gardens. "Are you going to hold that thing all day?"

Owain preened. "What can I say? I am a sword and shield man. The effect is useless without the shield."

"Most shield users have a way to carry them on their backs when not in combat," she muttered.

Fawx and Soren snickered behind her. She even saw Ronan's dimples make a rare appearance. Owain huffed and settled his shield on his back. She smiled to herself.

At the entrance of the back gardens, they gathered around the king and his footman. They were the first group to arrive.

"Have you chosen a team leader?" the king asked.

"Myra," a trio of voices chorused in unison.

She looked to Ronan, the one who hadn't chimed in. The look in his jade-green eyes was full of confidence as he nodded to her.

She shrugged at her father. "Me it is."

He waved at the footman, who held a bag. "Draw a tile for your flag color and entry position."

19

She held her breath as she stuck her hand in the bag. She'd never had great luck at this part. She pulled out the first tile she touched and grinned at the green three. Brown was the only better color for a flag. Myra waved the tile to her team. They all clapped and Fawx cheered. It was such a small victory, but their support made her feel amazing.

A servant gave them their green flag and showed them to a chalked-in three on the ground. They chatted quietly about potential strategies while waiting for the other teams to arrive. Finally, everything was ready, and her father stepped forward to give the last instructions.

"In capture the flag, the flag represents your country's highest official. Therefore, we have no specific guidelines as to how you must protect your flag. You may wish to guard it or hide it. You may even wish to take it with you. The only thing the flag cannot do is speak its mind." Her father chuckled. "Once you step through the barrier ahead, three things will happen. A protection spell will be placed upon each person. A defensive training spell will be placed on every weapon. And you will be teleported to your coordinating entry positions." He looked over the gathered crowd. "Let the battle begin!"

Everyone rushed forward, but Myra held her team back. She watched the opposition. When they were all through the barrier, she allowed her team to proceed. Fawx dashed ahead, Owain hot on his tail. Soren and Ronan stayed by her side, like two trees standing tall and steady. Her father winked at her as they entered the barrier.

One knife out cleaning his nails, Fawx casually leaned against one of many trees, while Owain surveyed the forested area ahead.

Soren lifted a branch aside. "Will the entire area be forested, Myra?"

"No. They'll have prepared a varied landscape: forest, caves, ruins, fort, river." She ticked off on her fingers. "Cliffs, canyons, waterfalls. Things like that."

"What do you want to do with our flag?" Ronan asked.

She tapped her chin. "I like to take the flag with me. It's not something most people do, and it's harder to steal."

Grinning, Fawx pulled off a leaf. "We can make a decoy."

"A single leaf will fool no one," Soren countered.

Myra held back a sigh and an eyeroll. If there was something to disagree on, those two would find it.

"I'm well aware." Fawx simpered at Soren, then turned his back. "May I borrow the flag, please, Myra?"

She smiled and handed it to him.

"If we use a decoy, someone will need to stay behind and act as a guard or the opposition will think it's a trap," Ronan said. "I'll do that."

Owain swung his shield off his back and banged it against a tree. "Oh, no. What do you think this is for?" He caught Myra's gaze and held it. "I am the ultimate defender."

She clenched a fist behind her back to keep from laughing —or yelling, she wasn't sure which. "We haven't even decided on our attack strategy yet. I might need either or both of you for that." She looked between Owain and Ronan. "Why don't the two of you come up with a decoy guard rotation for everyone?"

Owain nodded. "Everyone except you."

Her stomach knotted. "What do you mean, except me?"

Ronan answered softly, "You won't be part of the guard rotation."

Her voice deepened. "Why not?" Her head whipped between the two of them. "I know you haven't seen my fighting skills yet, but I'm here for more than show!"

From his spot at the foot of a tree, Fawx added, "That's not what they're saying, Myra."

She whirled around, chest heaving. "Then what am I missing?"

Soren, who had a scroll of paper and piece of charcoal out, answered, "A decoy with you guarding it won't work. Our opponents would never believe we'd leave you alone." He glanced up from his drawing, cat smile in full force. "Which is precisely why you should be the one to carry the flag. They won't suspect it."

She took a deep breath and slowly released it and her anger. She breathed in deeply one more time, looking at her four teammates, grateful for the different perspective they'd just given her. Maybe her parents hadn't been so wrong to push this on her.

Fawx bounced up, waving a green flag in each hand. "All done!"

Owain went over to check it out, curving around Myra. "Impressive. From over there, I couldn't tell them apart." '

Fawx faked a curtsy. "Why thank you, Your Gracelessness. What kind of tailor would I be if I couldn't whip up a flag in a few minutes?"

Owain cuffed him on the back of the head. "I've told you not to call me that."

"You're a tailor?" Myra asked.

He winked. "It's a hobby. My dear cousin doesn't allow me a true profession."

She felt her view of him expanding as all the pieces she knew rearranged themselves in her mind. She tucked the original flag into her tunic, leaving a corner visible for fairness. Although, since she had chosen to wear a green tunic and trousers this morning, it blended in quite well.

"Where shall we place our decoy?" she asked.

"Somewhere visible, but not easily accessible," came Soren's contribution.

"Also, the one on guard duty shouldn't be too hard to spot, so it doesn't feel like a trap," Ronan added.

The princess looked around and nodded to herself. "That just leaves one place: up a tree." She grinned. "I'll take it. I can check which battlefield layout they used while I'm up there."

As she expected, three of them strongly, loudly objected. While they were hotly arguing, Ronan pulled her aside. He tied his rope around her waist and tucked the decoy flag in her belt.

He put his hands on her shoulders, his jade green eyes serious. "I assume you have experience?"

She raised an eyebrow and gave a nod.

He jerked his chin toward a tree. "Then go before they notice. And be careful."

She picked her tree and asked Ronan for a boost. Instead of extending a knee for her to step on as she was expecting, he placed his hands on her waist and lifted her above his head. Her heart jumped into her throat, and she scrambled onto the branch in front of her. She stammered her thanks down to him, gave her heart a moment to settle, and —when it didn't— continued climbing, thoughts scattered. No one had ever touched her like that in such a casual setting. Her hand drifted down to her waist. And no one's touch had left such an impression before.

She shook herself. Ronan wasn't part of her parents' game. He wasn't an available choice.

At the top of the tree, she leaned her head back against the trunk, eyes closed. She inhaled and held her breath for the count of five. She opened her eyes, blew out her held breath, and nodded. Taking out a couple slim nails and a foldable hammer from her belt pack, she secured the decoy flag to the tree trunk, then scanned the horizon for landmarks. Hills to the north, crumbling tower to the west. Lowlands to the south and east.

She called down to Ronan. "Are you holding your end of the rope?"

"Yes, of course," he yelled back.

"And your footing is secure?"

"Yes."

She heard the question in his tone but ignored it.

"Good. I'm coming down."

She untied the rope from her waist, wove it around the trunk and her current branch, and retied it around herself. She jumped down, skipping two branches. The rope wrenched taut as she landed. She grinned and jumped again.

"Myra!" Ronan grunted as she landed. "Stop jumping. The rope's not long enough."

He waved the tail of the rope. She sat with a huff, close enough to see him clearly, but too far to jump safely to the ground. She watched him staring up at her, his chest heaving while a muscle in his jaw twitched. Was he . . . angry?

"Call the others over. You can all catch me."

"Absolutely not."

She inhaled. Counted to three. Tilted her head. Smiled.

"I meant if I fall. I'll climb down properly the rest of the way."

He looked up at her, at the tree, at the rope in his hands. His tensed shoulders loosened, but that muscle in his jaw still ticked.

"Fawx! Soren, Owain," he called. "Myra needs us."

The three halted mid-bickering and rushed over.

"Are you a cat, Myra? Shall I rescue you from this tree?" Fawx winked.

She smiled and shook her head. "If anyone's a cat, it's the one in black behind you." She waited for Fawx to notice Soren, then continued, "Rescue is not necessary. All I need is for you to spot me as I climb down. The tree was" —she unknotted the rope around her waist— "taller than expected."

"Um, Princess," Owain called, kicking the base of the tree. "I may not be much help. Things that require steadiness tend to go poorly for me." His voice trailed off at the end.

"You'll do fine. I've climbed up and down hundreds of trees in my life and only slipped twice," she reassured as she moved down a branch. "Both of those times I wore a dress and tripped on the skirts."

From the branch beside her, Fawx whispered, "I see you could never be anything as common as a cat." He winked and scampered upwards.

"What are you doing?" she called after him.

"Freeing the rope."

"Why?"

Soren answered from below, "It could create suspicion and ruin our decoy, if we left it in the tree."

Myra's foot slipped as she swung from the last branch and she lost her grip. Owain turned to catch her but bumped the toe of his boot on a root. He landed face-first on the ground, breaking her fall with his back.

Fawx's laughter rustled the branches above. "His Gracelessness strikes again."

"I've told you not to call me that!" Then he muttered, half to himself, "I told him not to call me that."

Owain tried to roll over with Myra still on top. She scrambled off and extended a hand to help him up, but the panic in his sky-blue eyes had her backing away instead. He dusted off his pant legs and winced as he regained his feet.

Sitting two branches up, holding the coiled rope, Fawx taunted, "Fine, fine. Catch me and I'll stop."

"What?!"

"One, two, three. . ."

He released the rope into Owain's outstretched arms, swung down backwards off the branch, and dropped to the ground beside him with a grin. Fawx tried to lean his elbow on Owain's shoulder, but the blonde prince was enough taller that it was too awkward. Instead, Fawx leaned against Owain's side, arms folded with one foot crossed over the other ankle.

"If you two are done fooling around" —Soren pulled out his scroll and charcoal— "we should get on with our battle strategy." He held the charcoal out to Myra. "Would you please sketch the battlefield?"

She took the stick of charcoal and started drawing. "When Father announced there would be five teams, I knew there were only a handful of options for the layout. Most of our capture the flag battle simulation layouts are for two and four teams. And our court magicians don't like to create new spells." She shrugged. "When we popped up in the forest, that narrowed it down further into two possibilities." She tapped the square she'd drawn in the middle. "This is our forest area.

25

To the north are hills full of caves. To the east will be a fort. The south has a river. And in the west," she trailed off.

"What's in the west?" Ronan prodded.

She sneered. "It's the reason this is my least favorite layout: the ruins. The river is bad enough; it's so hard to predict what people will do with their flag. But the ruins. That's where the magicians get creative."

She glowered at Soren. He licked his lips and looked away. Ronan put a hand on her shoulder.

"What do you mean?"

"The structural stability is inconsistent, as well as the contents. Sometimes there's a bridge or a tower, but not always. Sometimes you can safely climb around the ruins, but again, not always. It's. . . frustrating."

Fawx chimed in. "Well, anyway, we should probably start by scouting our competitors. See if we can find where and how they're keeping their flags."

Everyone agreed and Myra continued, "Owain, are you up for taking the first decoy guarding shift? It should give your back a chance to recover from serving as my cushion."

He rubbed his back and flinched, but swiftly smiled, trying to cover it. "Yes, my shield and I will guard the decoy as if our very existence depended upon it." He bowed with a flourish.

Soren said, "I don't believe it will be necessary to go quite that far."

Myra gave them both a look. "The rest of us will scout in pairs. Fawx and Ronan, I'd like you to check out the north and east. Soren and I will go west and south."

Fawx pouted. "Why does *he* get to go with you, Myra?"

She stretched then patted him on the head. "Don't worry, my little fox. We'll rotate pairs throughout the day. I want to spend time with each of you." She looked into the eyes of each man for a few seconds, trying to ignore the thumping in her chest when she reached Ronan. "I know why you're all here. My parents and each of you have taken the first steps. Now it's my turn."

26

*****

Myra and Soren peered through the brush at the tower ruins ahead.

"Look. Their flag is up there." She pointed near the top of the tower and squinted. "I think it's above a balcony."

He let go of the bush, sat back, and closed his eyes. "Why did you choose me for this?"

"Huh?"

"I'm not a magician. I can't read spells, so I cannot tell from here how stable those ruins are." A razor-sharp edge hid under the velvety softness of his voice.

"That's not. . . I didn't . . . You're not a magician?"

He looked away. "No."

"But your uncle—"

"Is the Grand Archon, the leader of all magicians? Yes, and he utterly despises me, his worthless heir."

A muscle in his jaw ticked from his clenched teeth, and she suspected from held-back tears as well. She laid a hand on his shoulder. His deep brown eyes connected to her stormy blue ones.

"You are *not* worthless."

One corner of his mouth lifted, and he tucked a stray piece of her brown hair behind her ear, still staring into her eyes. Her stomach fluttered at his touch.

"I have not as yet proven that to you."

She lifted an eyebrow. "Then I suppose we'd better get on with it."

They laughed at that together and peered through the bushes once more. Three of the opposing team's members stood at the base of the tower. The remaining two emerged from a nearby door. Myra and Soren watched them talk in a circle, then four of them set off in different directions, leaving only one behind to guard the tower and flag. After observing the guard for a time, she tapped Soren on the arm and moved a few steps away.

"Let's get this flag while we're here." She grinned; her eyes lit up with anticipation. "He'll be easy to evade and there must be stairs inside. They didn't have ropes or climbing gear."

His Adam's apple bobbed. "It seems a little too easy. Perhaps it's a trap?"

"If we do it now, or come back later, will that make it any less of a potential trap?"

He looked up at the trees. Down at the ground. Over through the bushes toward the tower. And finally back at her. He shook his head.

"Then we're going now."

"As you wish, my lady."

The cat smile and muscle twitch were back. She glared at him but headed out anyway. Together, they silently navigated the surrounding area until they could see the base of the tower. There they saw an open doorway and the bottom of a stone staircase. She pointed at the stairs and beamed. He ignored her. They waited for the guard to circle the tower, then dashed across the open ground and inside.

As they crept up the spiraling stairs, she whispered, "See. Easy."

He continued ignoring her.

Halfway up, she bumped a loose stone off the center edge. It clattered to the ground. They waited a few moments but kept climbing when they didn't hear the guard below. She apologized, and again, there was no response from him.

Three-fourths of the way up, she whirled on him. "Are you seriously sulking?"

From his spot by the wall, he answered. "No. I don't do well with heights."

"Oh." Her eyes widened. "Oooohhhh. Why didn't you tell me before?"

The coldness in his eyes made her step back. She nearly lost her footing, but he grabbed her upper arm before she fell.

"It's something else that makes me worthless."

He stepped around her, sprinting to the top of the stairs. He froze at the open door, staring out at the stone balcony.

Myra paused in the doorway with him. "We all have weaknesses. They don't make us worthless." When he looked down at her, she smiled. "Wait here. I'll go get the flag."

She strode out onto the balcony, searching all around. Spotting the flag above her head, she jumped for it. And missed. She tried jumping again —and failed again— so next she tried climbing the wall. Also a failure. She gritted her teeth and looked for something to stand on.

"Soren," she called. "I'm so sorry. It's too high. I can't reach it. You'll have to come out here."

As he stepped onto the balcony, the door slammed shut behind him. The tower shuddered.

"No!" he cried.

He pushed and pounded on the door.

"It's locked."

"I'm afraid we have a bigger problem," she called.

When he turned, she gestured to the crumbling balcony railing. He flattened his back against the wall, beads of sweat dripping down his face, chest heaving rapidly. She could see his hands trembling and hear him swallowing. The tower's movement ceased, leaving little more than a ledge's worth of the balcony. She slid over to Soren and slipped her hand into his.

"Close your eyes." Her voice was strong and steady; he obeyed. "Good. Now, inhale. That's right, slowly. Hold it. And exhale. Once more."

She coached his breathing until he had it under control. He turned his head toward her and opened one eye a slit.

"You saved me, Myra. Thank you."

His closed his eye again and rested his head back against the wall. His body still trembled and the sweat beading off his forehead mingled with tears streaming down his cheeks. It was the most open —the most vulnerable— she'd seen him. And she had a hunch there was more than a simple fear of heights in play.

"You're worth saving, Soren."

Her hand ached from how tightly he gripped it, but she didn't dare let go. With her other hand, she searched her belt bag for a spare cloth and wiped his face. He took one last shuddering breath before opening his eyes.

Forcing the velvet lightness back into his voice, he said, "My uncle would disagree with you."

"I highly doubt that. You are his family, after all."

With eyes unfocused and cast heavenward, he shook his head. "Not family. A useless piece of non-magical waste."

"Has he ever said that?"

The deadness in his eyes chilled her to core. "All the time. I am intimately familiar with high ledges, Myra. From the age at which my magical ability should have presented itself until I reached seventeen years —and gained the physical ability to defend myself— my uncle punished me by locking me out on a ledge for hours and days at a time." She gasped. "At first, he thought if I were scared enough, it would awaken the latent power. Later . . ."

She squeezed his hand. He returned the gesture.

"Later, he did it to vent his frustration and anger at my nothingness."

"Do you still have that scroll of paper from earlier?"

He pulled it out of his tunic with furrowed brows and passed it to her. One-handed, she clumsily unrolled it, ignoring her diagram of the battlefield layout, and pointed to the drawing above. It was a beautiful charcoal sketch of her.

"I noticed this before. Would a worthless person be able to draw something this stunning in the few minutes it took you?"

He tried to protest. She stuck the precious drawing back into his tunic.

"Plus, I thought *I* was good at strategy, but you saw the holes in my plans, and this trap." He opened his mouth, but she covered it with her hand. "You're not useless or worthless or nothing. You are helpful and valuable and unique. And right now, I need you."

He grabbed her wrist and pulled her to his chest, embracing her. He rested his head against the top of hers and whispered his thanks into her hair. Wide-eyed, she listened to his heart beating a fast, but steady rhythm. Hers felt like it had jumped into her throat and the bottom of her stomach simultaneously.

She cleared her throat and swiveled back beside him. "How about we get that flag now?"

He reached above her head and yanked it down.

"Show off," she muttered.

He smirked and tucked it inside his tunic. "How are we going to get down?"

She swung the pack off her back. "This is why I always bring rope."

His hand trembled as he pushed his black hair off his forehead. "You expect me to climb?"

Myra held his gaze. "No. I need you to be my anchor, Soren. There's nowhere to tie the rope. Once I'm down, I'll come back and unlock the door for you."

"And the guard?"

With a fiendish gleam, she patted her hand scythes. "Do I look helpless?"

*****

After getting herself and Soren down from the tower, and a short scuffle with the guard from the ruins team in between, they'd had an uneventful trip down to the river area in the south. They'd both agreed that the patch of unattended, freshly turned soil was a sure sign of a trap and headed back to the decoy tree for the rendezvous. There, the team converged, shared intel, and divided again.

Now, Myra headed back to the river trap with Owain trailing his usual distance behind her. She'd sent Soren with Fawx to the caves and hoped she wouldn't regret that pairing with the way those two tended to argue. She sighed to herself. It couldn't be helped. Fawx was still way too antsy for guard duty, and she was determined to get some answers about Owain's odd distance with her. And subjecting Ronan to another round of Fawx's antics seemed unfair, especially to the only man who was here as a favor to her and *not* as a part of her parents' plotting.

31

Owain yanked her arm, pulling her back under cover. He let go so fast that he overbalanced and fell on his hind end. She offered her hand, but he waved it off as had become customary. He stepped an extra three paces away from her and jutted his chin forward.

"I thought you said this was a river? That looks more like a stream."

In answer, she raised an eyebrow at him.

He scuffed his feet and cleared his throat. "What is our plan?"

She glanced out at the water and the patch of freshly turned soil on the other side, crossed her arms, and stared back at him.

"I can't go into battle with someone that doesn't trust me."

His arms hung loose at his sides and his jaw slackened. He avoided her fierce blue gaze.

"I do not understand."

"There must be a reason you maintain such a strict and noticeable distance from me."

The angel prince roughly scratched the back of his head, ruffling his blond hair.

"It's a curse," he mumbled.

"I'm sorry, what?"

He growled. "The clumsiness —*my* clumsiness— is a curse."

When he finally met her gaze, the underlying bitterness in his sky-blue eyes burned twisting tunnels of acid through her middle. She clutched her stomach and staggered back half a step.

"What kind of curse?"

"Every time I get close to a woman, I lose every ounce of agility and grace I possess and become a complete and utter klutz."

She pursed her lips. "That doesn't sound so bad."

He glowered. "Do you know how absolutely impossible it is to avoid women when you are a handsome prince?!? Or how humiliating it is to go from being the most graceful man

32

alive to earning the nickname 'His Gracelessness'?" He flung his hands up. "When I am alone or with a group of men, I'm the same as I have always been, but put a woman near me, and I trip on air. It is an impossible way to live."

Myra rubbed her chin, trying to decide which pressing question to ask first. "Have you tried to break the curse?"

"Have I tried to break the curse?" he muttered. "Have I *tried* to break the curse!? It has been five years! I've lost count of how many times I have 'tried to break the curse'," he snapped.

She glared and stalked deliberately toward him. He backed away, step for step, until his back hit a tree. The familiar panic passed through his eyes as she closed the gap between them.

She shook her finger in his face. "Don't you yell at me. I need to understand so I can help." She backed a few paces away and Owain slid to the ground. "How do you break it?"

He scrubbed his hands over his face and mumbled the answer into his palms. "True love."

After a few deep breaths, she said, "Expound."

"I must prove I have learned the true meaning of love."

"You broke someone's heart, didn't you?"

A small, sad smile flitted across his handsome face. "The wrong someone."

She squatted down and caught his eye. "If you choose to live your life with no regrets, the key is to like the person you are today and the one you are becoming tomorrow. In that case, there are no 'wrong people' in your past, for they have each had an influence on who you are right now."

He tried to look away, so she moved in close and grabbed his chin. "*You* have to decide every day if you like yourself, but from what I've seen, you're a good person. You're thoughtful and considerate. Sure, maybe you're a bit flashy and arrogant, but everyone has faults, or things they want to improve." She patted her chest. "I tend to speak my mind without thinking it through fully."

She backed away again and sat cross-legged on the ground, turning to keep one eye on him and the other on the buried flag across the narrow river. The silence stretched on between them and bled into their surroundings. Ever so slowly, Owain inched his way next to her.

In a whisper, he said, "It is most definitely a trap. It's too quiet here."

Her head bobbed in agreement. "We've been still long enough that there should have been some movement from the wildlife if we were the only ones in the area."

"What should we do?"

She grinned. "I thought you'd never ask."

Moments later, after a hasty explanation, she bolted into the open, sprinting top speed at the river. Myra leapt. She cleared the water, landed in a roll, and was up on her feet running to the turned-up soil all before Owain could voice his objections to her plan. Before she started digging, she waved him over with a glare. He blinked and took his first few steps. She smiled and turned her back, trusting that he would do his part and watch it while she unburied the flag.

Metal rang out against metal as she dug, scooping coarse dirt beside her like a dog. What she wouldn't give for her foldable shovel! She blew a breath out her nose and dug harder and faster. Her fingers met cloth. She gripped hard and ripped it out with a triumphant shout, whirling around to find Owain. Her heart took off on a race of its own as her widened eyes focused solely on the glint of the sword slicing toward her. No time to pull out her scythes. No time to duck or dodge. No time for anything. No time at all. Time ceased, the silence deafening.

A second heart thumped near hers. A strong arm wrapped around her and blocked the blade with a shield. That clang restored her stolen senses, and she watched the angel prince flawlessly wield his sword and shield mere inches away from her, swiftly dispatching their opponents.

He panted beside her. "Why did they disappear?"

"It's part of the protection spells and makes the game more challenging. If you receive a killing blow, you return to the beginning after a ten-minute penalty." She wandered over to the stream to wash the dirt from her hands. "Thank you."

He sheathed his sword and put his shield away. "I think the curse is broken, Myra." He grabbed her hands. "Did you see me fighting? I neither tripped nor stumbled nor dropped my sword."

The hopefulness in his eyes and voice was too much. She pulled away and headed back to the decoy tree. He walked by her side.

She flashed him a smile. "I just have one question for you. How did you sleep last night?"

"How did I sleep? That first night was horrible. You should have that lumpy mattress burned. But last night?" Owain twirled and grinned when he didn't trip or bump into anything. "Last night was marvelous! It felt like sleeping on a cloud."

*****

"We've narrowed it down to one of those three caves near the top." Fawx pointed and winked.

"You've searched *all* of the other caves?" Myra blinked.

He waggled his eyebrows and twitched his nose. "Of course. But" —he interlaced his fingers and stretched— "no matter how I persuaded him, the Fruitless Frost refused to accompany me to those last three caves."

They stood at the bottom of the hill, gazing at the towering slope riddled with dark holes. The light of the early afternoon sun barely reached them. She shivered and scowled at her new friend.

"You mean Soren?"

He nodded.

"He has a fear of heights."

He clutched his belly and doubled over with laughter. She whacked him on the shoulder. He straightened immediately, silent and serious.

"I never thought *he'd* be afraid of anything." Fawx motioned to the hill. "Shall we?"

35

She nodded and started walking. The incline wasn't steep enough to need a rope or other climbing gear, but there were a few places where she was glad to have a helping hand.

"How long have you known Soren?"

"Since childhood. His Gracelessness, too. In fact, apart from the Honorable Taran Ronan, I've known most of your guests for years."

"Why do you do that? Call them names, I mean."

"They started it, back when we were kids." His usual smile held an undercurrent of bitterness. "They weren't very imaginative, though, were they? I was even scrawnier as a kid. Looked more like a fox." He wagged his hand at his face. "Fawx. Fox. It's all the same."

"But I thought—"

"That I'd opted to go by my family name because it suited me better?" He tsked. "No, I took what they teased and bullied me with and made it my own. But I never wanted to be someone who was stuck being known only by his family. I'm not ashamed of them, but I do want to be seen as an individual." His voice softened. "As Noah."

She stopped to catch her breath and take a sip of water. They'd made it halfway and the view of the forest was breathtaking. A bird flew out of the trees, its screeching cry echoing through the air. He ducked behind her, trembling fingers digging into her shoulders.

"Is that a ha-ha-ha-hawk?" he stammered.

"Yes," she confirmed. "Don't tell me you're afraid of hawks?"

He chuckled. "Terrified."

She peeled his fingers off one shoulder and rubbed her collarbone. "You know they don't hunt people, right?"

He wrapped his arms around her middle and buried his face against her back. "No, but sometimes they hunt foxes."

She rotated just enough to be able to pat him on the back. "You may act a lot like a fox, Noah, but you're still a human."

He snorted. Then giggled. Then threw his head back and laughed until tears streamed down his freckled cheeks.

36

Still clinging to her, he said, "Thank you, Myra. I do know I'm a person, but it's nice to know someone else sees it, too."

She looked away from the earnestness in his golden-brown eyes, butterflies churning her insides from cream to butter. She peeked back at him and those butterflies fluttered up by her heart, trying to escape her chest. She took off up the hill. A few moments later, his hand slid into hers. She glanced his way. He flashed his usual wink.

"One of my pranks backfired when I was thirteen," he said. "I ended up getting stuck as a fox for three weeks before they found me. Hawks are common where I grew up." He bit his lower lip and smiled. "Been terrified of them ever since."

"That's understandable." She squeezed his hand. "Who were you trying to play pranks on?"

He shuddered as the distant hawk screed again. "They're a couple years older than me, you know. The Dark Nephew and the Bright Princeling."

"Soren and Owain?"

An affirmative grunt. "I was angry and helpless and hurt. And so alone." He stopped walking and stared, unseeing, out over the forest. "My parents had just died, and my cousin had brought me to her court. There they were, my childhood tormentors —the ones who'd stripped my individual identity from me— being treated as angels." His voice became scratchy. "I wanted them to know what it felt like to lose their humanity."

She rubbed his back. He turned to her, sorrow and regret brimming in his eyes. He closed them for a moment, and when he opened them again, the mischievous sparkle had returned. Except for the single tear that carved a silent trail down his freckled cheek.

"Instead, I decided to embrace the fox life, be friends with everyone, and have fun. It suits me, don't you think?"

He tucked his hands under his chin and tilted his head with a cheeky grin.

37

She smiled back, nodded, and tugged him uphill. He slipped his hand back into hers and she had to admit, it was comfortable —and comforting— to hold his calloused hand.

He sighed.

"What is it?" she asked.

"I know being 'Fawx' fits, and I'm happy being who I am, but sometimes I miss being 'Noah'."

They stopped outside the first of the top three caves.

"Are you certain no one's in there?" she asked.

He nodded. "Ronan and I saw them leave when we first scouted out the place, and every cave has been completely empty with no signs of human interference. It does make me wonder what they and the other teams have been doing all day, though. It's odd that we haven't run into anyone else at all. Something feels off."

"I've been thinking that myself. Let's hurry here and get back to the others."

Fawx held her back. "Before we do, I have to ask, how am I doing?"

"What?"

"It is a competition, Myra." He winked. "Compared to your other choices, how am I doing?"

She pursed her lips. "Let me answer your question with one of my own: how did you sleep last night?"

He grinned. "Barely a wink. Are all the mattresses in your home unbearably lumpy or just the ones for guests? I ended up sleeping on the floor, instead. It was more comfortable."

*****

When Myra and Fawx arrived at the decoy tree after getting the cave flag, they found Soren bound and gagged at the base of the trunk. He was a bit disheveled —and looked like a cat primed to hiss and spit— but unharmed. Ronan and Owain returned as Fawx was cutting his ropes.

"What happened?" Myra asked.

"I was tackled from behind while one climbed for the decoy and the rest stood guard. There were more than five." His velvet voice was lined with steel.

38

She shared a look with Fawx.

"The other teams must've joined forces," Fawx said.

"And when they realized it was a decoy?" Myra asked.

Soren shook his head. "The climber took it with him. He, at least, is continuing the charade."

She hummed in thought.

"There is another matter," Soren said.

All eyes on him, but his remained fixed on the ground. His throat bobbed, and he breathed deep.

"After they restrained me, I was searched. They took the tower flag."

Owain hissed a curse. Myra ground her jaw back and forth, until boiling rage burst from the pit of her stomach in a guttural scream. She spun away, acid tears burning a course down her cheeks, muscles locked in tense rigor. Her trembling legs gave out, and she plopped to the ground. A shuffle of dry, fallen leaves and someone sat beside her.

"Don't be too hard on Soren," Ronan said.

She looked at him out of the corner of her eye. "I'm not angry at Soren. It's clear that he was ambushed and grossly outnumbered."

Soren sat on the other side of her. "You sound confident of that assessment."

She stared him down, then nodded at his curved blade. "The swordsmiths who make those only give them to persons who have proven their battle prowess. If you'd had any chance to unsheathe it, you wouldn't have been tied up when we got here."

"You know a lot about my sword."

She tapped her hand scythes. "My instructor has a sword like yours."

Fawx and Owain sat in front, rounding out the circle.

Fawx nudged her foot. "Then why are you upset?"

"I'm disappointed in myself. You all put your faith in me as your leader, and I let you down. I didn't see this coming; the other teams joining forces. What's worse is that it's a strategy *I've* used before!"

Ronan laid his hand on top of hers. "Sorry, Myra. I think we put too much pressure on you, expecting you to make all the decisions. That's not what good teammates do."

The warmth of his hand on hers accompanied by the kindness in his jade green eyes caused a matching heat to simmer in her chest. Her eyes flitted over to Fawx. A rock tumbled through her stomach at his expression. She closed her eyes and swallowed. Why had her parents thought this was a good idea?

Owain spoke, unknowingly breaking the tension inside her. "Ronan and I think all the other teams have gathered at the fort."

She smiled at him, stood, and brushed off her pants. "Then that's where we're headed. We can make a plan when we see what's there."

*****

They stopped at the edge of the forest. After a short argument with Myra, Fawx climbed a tree for a better view of the inside of the fort. He'd brought a pair of binoculars.

"They have the tower flag and our decoy up on two corners of the battlement," he called down from his perch. "The fort flag is on a pole in the middle of the grounds. All the doors are closed, except for a small side door on the north wall. Could be a trap. It's most likely a trap." He counted under his breath. "All twenty of our opponents are spread throughout the fort. Looks like there are two guards per flag and the rest of them are roaming around."

She sighed and checked the level of the sun in the sky. "Late afternoon. Not too long until sunset, but there should be plenty of time for us to get the last two flags if you want to. Or we can stick with the three that we have. Three is enough for a victory."

"What do *you* want to do, Myra?" Ronan asked.

She twisted her lower lip. "I've never had such talented teammates before, nor been this close to a clean sweep." Her eyes sparkled. "Let's go for it."

40

Three out of four readily agreed while Ronan released a small sigh before adding his consent. She beamed at her teammates and gathered them close around, laying out a detailed plan of attack using everyone's strengths to the best of her abilities. Although, she kept Ronan to herself. She'd hardly spent any time with him all day.

On hands and knees, she and Ronan slowly crawled through tall grass to the opposite side of the fort. She'd sent the other three to sneak in through the open northern door. Once inside, two would recapture the tower flag and the third would open the eastern door for her and Ronan.

She dropped behind and tugged on his ankle. "So, what does my inside man think of my options?"

He looked over his shoulder at her, one eyebrow raised. "What do *you* think of them?"

She chewed on her lips and caught back up. "Owain's a decent man, but he's not the right fit for me. He's a bit" —she hummed— "much."

Ronan snorted and tried to hide a smile. It made his jade green eyes shine and his dimples pop.

"Soren is . . ."

"Not who everyone thinks he is," he interrupted. "He's dangerous, Myra. You can't trust him."

"What do you mean? How can you tell?"

"This isn't my first encounter with Grand Archon Marius' son."

"You mean nephew. Soren is Marius' nephew."

Ronan stopped crawling to look into her eyes. "No. Soren is his son. But the Grand Archon of all mages couldn't possibly have a non-magical son, could he? Very few know the truth. I'm not even sure if Soren knows."

Myra swallowed and continued moving. "How do you know?"

"My mentor used to be a renowned midwife. Soren's birth had complications, so they called for her. He barely survived; his mother didn't."

"And your mentor told you this?"

He shook his head. "When I was maybe fifteen, an angry kid came looking for her, blaming her for taking away his magic. He was only twelve or thirteen, but he was filled with so much hate and rage. He tried to kill her. After he left, she told me the story of his birth." He sighed. "The darkness I saw in him that day, it's still there."

She crawled in silence for a few moments. "Maybe it's the darkness of a child that grew up without love. Not the darkness of one who inflicts pain on others."

"Perhaps." His voice softened as he continued, "But I don't want to take that chance with you."

The simmering heat returned to her chest and expanded to her cheeks.

"That just leaves Fawx," she said.

A flash of his wink flitted through her mind, accompanied by fluttering in her stomach. She didn't want to talk about Fawx with Ronan.

"And me."

Her upper arms gave out. In a hushed tone, she asked, "Are you an option?"

"I'd like to be, if you'll have me."

She closed her eyes. "How did you sleep last night?"

His low chuckle sent shivers down her spine. "A little better, though not as well as at home. The servants changed the mattress, but the new one was still a bit lumpy."

"Can you bear with it for one more night?"

"For you I'd be willing to endure many uncomfortable things, Myra. Including lumpy mattresses." He nudged her shoulder. "You are unlike any woman I have ever met. Intelligent, brave, bold, and beautiful."

He tucked a stray wisp of her dark brown hair behind her ear, licked his lips and leaned in. The simmering heat exploded into a raging inferno accompanied by the drumbeat of her heart. She desperately wanted to let his lips connect with hers, but one question held her back. She pulled away.

"Would your people approve?"

"Huh?"

"Would the citizens of the city-state of Dinas Tov approve of their Taran marrying a crown princess?"

After several moments of silence, he answered, "I don't know."

She resumed crawling. "Did you always want to be the Taran?"

"I never wanted to be Taran. My mentor nominated me for the last election and the people chose me. I do my best for them every day."

"I've heard that it's a lifelong position, like a king, even though you've been elected by popular vote?"

"Yes. I'll be the Taran until I die."

The sadness in his eyes caused a lump to form in her throat. She put her hand on his arm.

"You said you didn't want to be the Taran. What did you want to be?"

His half-smile highlighted a dimple. "I was going to be a travelling doctor."

She looked him over thoughtfully. "That explains why a political leader had a midwife for a mentor. And why you think all problems are solvable."

He shushed her, eyes flicking to the wall above. They'd reached their destination and now sounds of a scuffle echoed down. A knife dropped beside Myra. She looked up in time to catch a wink from Fawx. Two minutes later, he was grabbing his knife and running back inside through the newly opened door. He'd also managed to sneak in a peck on her cheek.

"I guess that's our cue," she said.

Ronan nodded and together they stepped into the doorway.

All the color drained from her face. Her teammates had gotten the two missing flags, but now the three of them were backed into a corner, penned in by the combined forces of the other teams.

"We have to help them," she whispered, wide-eyed.

She pulled out her hand scythes and took three determined steps forward. A wooden stick across her chest yanked her back into Ronan's arms. He held his staff firm, not giving an inch as she struggled.

"Why?"

"If you rush out there without a plan, you'll end up getting into the same mess," he answered.

A man stepped out of the shadows, pointing a sword at her throat. "He's right, you know. You're in quite a mess, Princess."

He motioned them forward. Ronan dropped his staff to the side, releasing Myra. She flexed her scythes.

"Ah, ah, ah. Don't even think about it." The sword-holder called over his shoulder, "And why don't you gentlemen go ahead and put your weapons down as well."

Myra watched, helpless, as Owain, Soren, and Fawx dropped their weapons. Her hands tightened on hers and fury flashed through her stormy blue eyes. The sword tip slid uncomfortably close to her skin.

"Search them for those flags."

She stared her captor down, chest heaving, as the day's hard work disappeared in the blink of an eye.

*****

Myra knocked on Soren's door.

"Come in," his velvet soft voice answered.

"Sorry to disturb you. There was a question I forgot—"

She stopped when she saw the tiny rocks in his hand, though he tried to hide them behind his back. She bit her lip and backed out the door.

"Guess that answers that. Ronan was right; you can't be trusted."

He tossed the gravel on the floor with a growl. "Myra, wait! I can explain."

But she'd already turned the corner.

*****

One last morning. One last breakfast. One last announcement from her father. She glanced sidelong down the table at the two men on the other side of her mother. The two men that had once again passed last night's pea gravel test.

Acid gripped her heart and she couldn't breathe. How was she supposed to choose?

"As you can see, we have our final two candidates," the king said. "The last test will be a private one. It is a sacred family tradition that's been passed down for generations. I hope you all understand." He motioned to Fawx and Ronan. "If you will follow me, please?"

They passed her, Ronan with a head nod, Fawx with a blown kiss and a wink. She pulled her mother aside.

"I want to take the test."

"What's that, darling?"

"I need to do the test, too, Mother. Please? I need to know."

Her mother looked her square in the eyes.

"All right, darling. I understand." She smiled. "Follow me."

They entered a room with five beds. Five tall, fluffy beds with stepping stools beside them.

Her mother said, "Each bed has twenty mattresses and twenty comforters. Only one bed has one piece of pea gravel underneath everything. If you can feel it, you are a true princess." She turned to her daughter. "But, darling, you don't need this silly test to prove that."

"If I expect it of my life partner, I expect it of myself."

Myra climbed onto the first bed. Nothing. She left an impression of her body in the fluff. Second, third, and fourth beds also nothing. She looked up at the last bed and swallowed the lump of lead down to the pit of her stomach. Fifth bed. Like lying on clouds, same as the others. Except. She wriggled. How was that even possible? There's no way that rock was on the bottom. And a single piece of pea gravel? She shuddered. It felt like a boulder.

She sat up and looked under her back. Hopped down and reached under the mattress. She stared at the tiny pebble, jaw slack. Her mother's arm wrapped around her shoulders.

"Do you believe me now?"

*****

She sat in the room of beds with a mask covering her entire face. The maids had fluffed them again to remove the

45

evidence of which beds she had lain in and her mother had replaced the pea gravel. She could watch but had to remain perfectly still and silent.

Her mother stood in the doorway with Fawx. "If you would, please, try all the beds and let us know which is the most comfortable. We know you've had a terrible time sleeping here."

He flourished a bow. "It would be my pleasure, Your Majesty."

"Thank you, Lord Fawx." The queen shut the door.

Fawx dashed by Myra and jumped on the fifth bed. He made a disgusted noise in the back of his throat.

"Really, Myra, are all the mattresses in your castle lumpy?"

"You know I'm not supposed to talk to you, right?"

He sprung down and grabbed her hands, squatting to match her eye level. He tilted his head, fluttered his eyelashes, and smirked.

"But that's how I know you love me."

Then he was off to the next bed. He moaned in pleasure.

"I see I was wrong. What a heavenly cloud!" He yawned and curled up on his side. "I'll just take a little nap."

She sighed and walked over to that bed, resting her chin on top of the stacked mattresses.

"What is your dream for the future?"

His golden-brown eyes popped open. "You are, Myra."

Warmth fluttered and spread through her chest. Her mischievous fox was all serious for once. She bit her lower lip.

"No, I mean, before we met. What was your dream?"

He rolled on his back and flung an arm over his eyes. "Oh, that. Freedom."

"You're not free? But your cousin is the Empress."

"Exactly. The Empress controls every aspect of my life. Do you know why I know everyone?"

She shook her head before remembering he had his eyes covered. "No."

"I'm one of her spies, Myra. Because no one suspects the playful, friendly Fawx."

46

He brought his hands up by his cheeks in fake paws and smiled a bitter smile. He rolled onto his stomach and rested his chin in his hands.

"I'm not a way to freedom."

"You're right and wrong." He laughed at her furrowed brows. "It's true that marrying a crown princess would be a different kind of cage, but if I lived in that cage with you, the bars would expand and the whole world would fit inside." One long blink later, with tears slipping down his cheeks, he said, "It would be worth it, to spend my life with you."

"Noah," she whispered, her own mirrored tears sliding down.

He winked and jumped down. Standing behind her, he whispered in her ear, "I know I'm not your first choice, but I'll stay. I'll be your backup prince."

He turned to leave. She grabbed his hand.

"Aren't you going to try the other beds?"

He shook his head. "You and I both know I passed the test."

*****

Ronan entered the room of beds after receiving the same instructions that Fawx had. He took a different approach and tried the middle bed first. Myra remained silent, thinking over Fawx's declaration. She watched the quiet, methodical man in front of her. What would his people say? And what would he do if his people said no? She held her breath as he climbed into the fifth bed. It was a moot point if he failed this test.

He shifted his neck and shoulders. Then rolled from one side onto the other with a scowl. He huffed.

"I don't understand how something can be both comfortable and immeasurably uncomfortable at the same time." He looked at her. "Is this the test?"

She pulled her mask off, grinning and nodding. "And you passed."

He climbed down and she smacked his shoulder. He winced.

"Why did you stop me yesterday? We lost everything because you stopped me."

"One, you don't know what might have happened. Two, the flags were not the most important part of the game."

She cracked her jaw. "What do you mean the flags weren't the most important? It's called 'capture the flag'?"

"True, but it's a battle simulation and at the end of the day, *you* are a political leader. *You* are what the flags represent. Countless times throughout the day you chose to put yourself in harm's way because it was 'just a game'. That's a dangerous attitude. What you do in practice becomes habit. When you're faced with a real-life crisis, habits are what you rely on."

Through clenched teeth, she said, "I can take care of myself."

"I know you can. I watched you do it."

Her face scrunched up in such confusion that he laughed.

"Your court magicians recorded the game on crystals. I watched it last night with the others." He ran his fingers through her hair. "And every time you threw yourself into danger, my heart threatened to stop. I'm not telling you to stop fighting. That would be a waste of your talents and it would destroy a piece of your soul. I want you to think before you jump into action."

"I could work on that." She smiled, warmth spreading from her chest throughout her limbs. "What about your people?"

His dimpled smile answered. "I'll have to ask them, which means holding an election."

"And if they say no?" she whispered at the floor.

He turned away. "Then I'll abide by their decision. I'm their Taran. My people come first."

*****

Myra stood with her parents in an upper hallway looking out a window at the sheep field. Ronan stood petting the sheep, staring at the sky. Fawx was curled up under the tree, napping.

"So, they both passed the test, eh?" her father asked.

She nodded.

"From what I've seen, either would make a fine husband," her father said.

Again, she nodded.

Her mother held her hand and patted it. "There's no rush, darling. Follow your heart."

After a hug, her parents walked off, hand-in-hand, leaving her alone at the window. Myra looked down at the scene below, a slow smile curving her lips. *Follow my heart, hm? Yes, that's just what I'll do.*

About the Author

Lucina M. Huff was born and raised in the stunning and diverse PNW city of Tacoma, WA. Since marrying her own handsome prince charming, she has lived in more places than she cares to count. She is a stay-at-home mom of two spunky girls. She had two dreams while growing up: to be a mother and to be an author. She is pleased to be living both her dreams. Her hobbies include (but are not limited to): crocheting, playing the piano, chainmaille jewelry making, and bingeing all the stories.

Where to Connect:

Facebook Page - Lucina M. Huff
Instagram - lucinamhuff
authorlucinamhuff.com

Other books by Lucina M. Huff:

The Book of Memories

Made in the USA
Columbia, SC
27 June 2023

19359071R00030